| DATE DUE | | | |
|---|---|---|---|
| | | | |
| | | | |
| | | | |
| | | | |
| | | | |
| | | | |
| | | | |
| | | | |
| | | | |
| | | | |
| | | | |
| | | | |
| | | | |

413

"HELLO READING books are a perfect introduction to reading. Brief sentences full of word repetition and full-color pictures stress visual clues to help a child take the first important steps toward reading. Mastering these storybooks will build children's reading confidence and give them the enthusiasm to stand on their own in the world of words."

—Bee Cullinan
Past President of the International Reading
Association, Professor in New York University's
Early Childhood and Elementary Education Program


"Readers aren't born, they're made. Desire is planted—planted by parents who work at it."

—Jim Trelease
author of *The Read-Aloud Handbook*


"When I was a classroom reading teacher, I recognized the importance of good stories in making children understand that reading is more than just recognizing words. I saw that children who have ready access to storybooks get excited about reading. They also make noticeably greater gains in reading comprehension. The development of the HELLO READING stories grows out of this experience."

—Harriet Ziefert
M.A.T., New York University School of Education
Author, Language Arts Module,
Scholastic Early Childhood Program

*For A.M.B.*

VIKING
Published by the Penguin Group
Penguin Books USA Inc.,
375 Hudson Street, New York, New York 10014, U.S.A.
Penguin Books Ltd, 27 Wrights Lane, London W8 5TZ, England
Penguin Books Australia Ltd, Ringwood, Victoria, Australia
Penguin Books Canada Ltd, 10 Alcorn Avenue, Toronto, Ontario, Canada M4V 3B2
Penguin Books (N.Z.) Ltd, 182-190 Wairau Road, Auckland 10, New Zealand

Penguin Books Ltd, Registered Offices: Harmondsworth, Middlesex, England

First published in 1993 by Viking Penguin, a division of Penguin Books USA Inc.

Published simultaneously in a Puffin Books edition.

1 3 5 7 9 10 8 6 4 2

Text copyright © Harriet Ziefert, 1993
Illustrations copyright © David Jacobson, 1993
All rights reserved
Library of Congress Catalog Card Number: 92-80383
ISBN: 0-670-84569-8

Printed in Singapore for Harriet Ziefert, Inc.

# THREE WISHES

**Harriet Ziefert**
**Pictures by David Jacobson**

VIKING

# Chapter One
# Morning Wish

I want to fish
in the pond
outside.

I want to put
my fishing line
in the water.

I want to pull…

and pull...

and pull.

And, before I'm done,
I want to pull out
two hundred…

and twenty-two fishes!

# Chapter Two
# Noon Wish

I want to be
boss of the kitchen...

and eat just how I want.

I'll sit at the head of the table.

I'll begin with raisins
and peanuts.

I'll end with french fries and pizza.

And, when I'm done,
I'll throw my napkin
away and...

I'll wipe my mouth
on my sleeve!

# Chapter Three

# Night Wish

I want to climb
the apple tree
outside my window.

I want to climb
the tree at night...

and get a piece of fruit…

and a piece of moon.

Then I will go to bed—
my pockets full—
one with fruit...

and the other
with moon.